SOLITARY TOES AND BROWN-HEADED COWBIRDS

A Hickory Doc's Tale

Written By
LINDA HARKEY

Illustrations By
MIKE MINICK

Archway Publishing books may be ordered through booksellers or by contacting:

Archway Publishing
1663 Liberty Drive
Bloomington, IN 47403
www.archwaypublishing.com
1 (888) 242-5904

ISBN: 978-1-4808-7316-2 (sc)
ISBN: 978-1-4808-7315-5 (e)

Print information available on the last page.

Archway Publishing rev. date: 01/30/2019

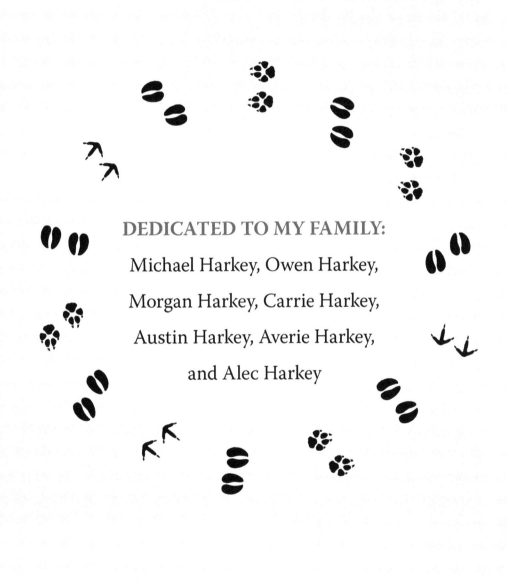

DEDICATED TO MY FAMILY:

Michael Harkey, Owen Harkey,

Morgan Harkey, Carrie Harkey,

Austin Harkey, Averie Harkey,

and Alec Harkey

"These hunting dogs jump off the page and come to life through Linda's tales of their adventures as they face challenges in life. I am a second grade teacher in Eagle Nest, New Mexico, and I also organize our public library summer reading program. Linda's stories engaged our students in the lives of these dogs sparking great discussions and learning activities about character development, sequencing, and elements of the story. One student brought a stuffed puppy dog named after Zeke to join the fun every week."

Cindy Carr
NBCT

"A lovable bird dog points the way to outdoor fun in country in this children's book......A sweet slice of rural American canine life."

Kirkus Review

"I had the opportunity to spend the summer doing a summer reading program in Northern New Mexico where we read Linda Harkey's book, Hickory Doc's Tales. When we got to the chapter, "Willie's First Secret", the kids loved it and eagerly wanted to figure out the "secret". The last paragraph revealed there were more secrets, so the kids wanted to know more stories about Willie. I am so excited that Willie's secrets will be revealed in this new children's book. I can't wait to enjoy it with my students!"

Dana McBee
4th-5th Grade Teacher

"Linda Harkey's Hickory Doc's Tales is full of adventure and mischief relayed from the perspective of animals. Its stories are silly and fun, even as they share important life lessons."

Foreword Review

"Everyone loves a good mystery. The chapter which is titled "Willie's First Secret" has such a mystery. Willie the crow works with Doc and Zeke to solve a mystery. There are some good vocabulary words that you could add to your spelling list for extra credit working with 3rd and 4th graders."

Mary Parker
retired elementary teacher

"Much of the book's charm lies in its unique, lovable narrator. When Newt, a Lab at the kennel, sadly realizes he's different from the others, Doc lists all his positive attributes. And he admits when he's erred, such as when he gobbled up all the food at a dinner party."

Blueink Review

BROWN-HEADED COWBIRD AND A DOVE

Months without rain left the scorched pastures of the Lazy Dog Hacienda covered with hundreds of tiny creatures people called grasshoppers. These are insects that use their strong back legs as springs to jump. The Great One calls this the off-season. This is the time in which birds rest, have their young, and eat grasshoppers. The Great One is our name for the one that takes us bird hunting.

So Zeke, my annoying brother, and I (better known as Doc) had to find other ways to fine tune our hunting skills. We spent most mornings entertaining ourselves with a game called "catch the jumping grasshoppers" - but not today. It was too hot!

Zeke and I are German Shorthaired Pointers. Our breed is known for hunting birds. Zeke's pedigree name is Windwalker Storm Shadow. He definitely fits the Storm Shadow part of his name. Zeke trembles, barks, and shows his teeth when

he gets mad, which is most of the time. The pack thinks that's pretty funny, since Zeke's teeth are really short nubs worn down by four years of chewing on wire fences and kennel runs.

Zeke always says, "Doc, the reason I chew on metal is that it leaves my teeth bright and sparkly in the sun." I have to admit he is right about that.

Zeke has a short ticked coat which means speckled liver (brown) and white. Personally, I've always felt that ticked dogs are more selfish and suspicious.

My pedigree name is Chicoree's Hickory Doc, but folks around here call me Doc. My bloodline can be traced back to Germany. My great-great-great-grandpa, Esser's Chic was the greatest champion hunting dog in Germany.

My coat is a solid liver color with white on my chest. I am the oldest and wisest of the pack, being five years old. The Great One expects me to keep the others in line, especially on hunting trips.

Now, where was I? Oh yes, Zeke and I were lying in the shade around the trunk of the big oak tree in the north pasture. We just finished our noon snack of leftover pizza the Other One (the mother of all mothers) had made.

I watched as a line of ants crawled across Zeke's protruding tummy. It rose and fell with his snoring. The ants would find out what I already knew. Zeke always licked every morsel of food off his body. He was notorious for gobbling down his chow, then pushing the pups aside to finish theirs.

Zeke rolled his eyes towards me, snorting and yipping. "Doc, there's no point in wasting energy today by trying to find birds. That causes us to pant."

Dogs don't sweat, so when it's this hot we're not able to use our skills of hunting and pointing birds. *Wuff, wuff,* I barked, "You're right Zeke, you can't smell through your nose while you breath through your mouth. But, don't forget Zeke, after all you ate, there's no way you're able to hunt birds anyway."

Zeke sat up on his haunches, squinted his eyes, and growled. "That's not right, Doc. I can always find birds! Why, I'm the fastest dog around." I scratched behind my ear. *Zeke is the same dog that walks with our hunter while we are out running, finding, and pointing birds. Then, Zeke trots up and pretends he found the birds.*

I cocked my head as I heard a strange shrill whistle, followed by chatter. "Zeke, did you hear that?"

Zeke snarled. "Doc, quit bothering me. You know I need my sleep. I worked hard this morning playing with the pups."

Disgusted, I barked "The only thing you did was gobble your chow down, and watch me work with the pups. Then you strolled down with the Great One to get the newspaper. After that you complained about the hot summer day and decided to sleep until lunch!"

Zeke yawned. "You remember it your way, and I'll remember it my way. What sound are you hearing, anyway?"

I rolled my eyes, then stared at Zeke. "Ah, it sounds like a bird. I just can't figure which one." I heard the whistle again.

"Yes, I hear it now. What bird is that?" Zeke looked puzzled as he raised up again and sat back on his haunches.

Flying in the sky toward our oak tree was a bird. I sat up and started howling. "It's a BROWN-HEADED COWBIRD!" I knew that because it had dark colors on its body and a brown head. We were trained at hunting school to recognize birds and learn their scent.

Zeke and I became excited. We jumped and howled as the cowbird landed in the dove's nest, right above us. Then I heard the shrill whistle and clicking sound the cowbird made — *wee, click, wee, click.*

Cowbird and dove feathers flew everywhere. After that came the soft sounds of *coo-ah, coo, coo,* from the gray colored dove. The cowbird shoved the dove out of its nest. Plop! It landed right on top of Zeke's head.

Zeke is not one to move at all unless he is motivated. Yep, he was motivated! Zeke jumped, twisted, nipped, and threw his head back and forth trying to get the dove off. The dove hung on and clamped down with its toes. However, that didn't last long because the dove slipped and ended up on Zeke's large brown nose. I was shaking with laughter so hard I couldn't bark. Eye-to-eye, head-to-head, both Zeke and the dove struggled. Feathers were flying, ears were flopping, and still Zeke continued to jump, twist, and nip until the dove finally let go and flew off. I heard the dove cooing. "When I get my beak on that cowbird….."

Cowbirds are too lazy to make their own nest. They just kick other birds out and then lay their eggs in those nests. The cowbird reminded me of Zeke – both looking out for themselves. As I was thinking this, Zeke still angry at the dove, growled. "Now I know why I like cowbirds. They don't work to make their own nests. The cowbirds just take another bird's nest."

A SWEATY SMELL

Just then, I heard CHUG, CHUG, KNOCK, KNOCK. That was the engine of our old red hunting truck with a trailer hitched to the back. It rounded the corner of the driveway.

"Zeke, surely it isn't time to go hunting. Our hunter takes us when the leaves begin to turn." I looked at Zeke. Zeke's gaze was fixed entirely on watching the truck. "Doc, that doesn't look like our dog trailer attached to the truck. Look how tall it is!"

Zeke was right. The trailer was long and tall like the swing set. The Great One got out and opened the trailer. Out came the biggest and longest brown dog in the world. After taking one whiff, I knew it wasn't a dog smell. It smelled sweaty, and dogs don't sweat – we pant.

We watched as our hunter put a very large leash around the head and long neck of the creature. He brought it towards us, took the leash off and left. Now we were all alone with the creature.

Zeke's hair stood straight up on his back. He growled and barked. Then he backed up and crouched behind the hay bale. He figures the dog that's in front will get the challenge first – not the one in back. There I was, alone, trembling, and looking up at a huge brown creature that could squash me with only one of its strange looking paws.

Zeke pulled himself slowly back to me. He realized the creature wasn't going to attack us when it trotted directly to the hay bale and began eating.

Zeke yipped softly, "Doc, the creature is eating hay. Dogs don't eat hay. Look at its paws. Those are definitely not dog paws. We have toes on our paws. Wait a minute. Doc, look, it has solitary toes. What is this creature?"

I looked up at it and then back at Zeke. I sat down on my haunches and started scratching behind my ears. "Well, Zeke, let's find out." *I was beginning to think Zeke actually liked this creature. It had gone directly for its chow, the hay bale. Zeke could identify with that.*

Zeke shook all over. His eyes got as big as those tennis balls the Great One throws to us. "Doc, you're the oldest. You ask, I'll watch."

Sure you will. I crept closer to the head of the creature and let out a short, loud, cry of *woof, woof.* "The people call us Doc and Zeke." I glanced around for Zeke. He wasn't there. Nope, Zeke was running towards the people's house. Now, it was just the creature and me!

I stood as tall as a dog can, with four paws planted firmly on the ground. "What are you called and what kind of creature are you? We are hunting dogs, but I know you're not!"

The creature continued eating the hay, but turned its head towards me. Finally, after chewing even longer than Zeke, the creature neighed, *hee, hee, heeee.* "I am B. J., the famous mare quarter horse. Surely, you've heard of me. I have won many races. But, I'm retired now and your hunter brought me here to help him hunt birds."

"Hunting birds!" I howled as loud as I could, hoping my brother would hear and come back. Sometimes even Zeke does the right thing. I heard Zeke's howling and yelping as he came running towards me. He brought one reinforcement from the pack, Deacon, our three-legged German Shorthaired Pointer.

Deacon was white with brown spots and known as the fastest dog in the pack. He was also the smartest hunting dog we had - next to me. That's because Deacon loved to eat the binding off books. Not just any book, but only the Great One's hunting journals. Deacon would always say, "Doc, you can learn a lot about a book by eating the binding." Deacon called that a short-cut to reading.

I knew that with our reinforcement of Deacon, we would be able to handle B. J.

B. J. looked up and saw Zeke and Deacon running towards her. She became panicky, pitched her black mane, bared her teeth, pawed the ground, reared her forelegs, and let out a shrill whinny, *HEE, HEEEEE.*

Deacon and Zeke stopped dead in their tracks. I watched B. J. rear up, then start towards me. I made the same move Zeke usually does. I backed away from B. J. and came closer to Zeke and Deacon. *Surely I am not becoming more like my brother.* I stopped, turned, faced B. J., snarled, bared my teeth, and growled. "The pack does the hunting around here – not horses!"

B. J. stopped right before reaching us. She blew air in and out of her huge nostrils, then pawed the ground with those solitary toes. B. J. was definitely glaring at us. She neighed. "As I was saying before, I am B. J. the famous quarter horse, and your hunter wants to hunt birds with me!"

"Well", Zeke growled as he moved back behind me. "You need paws to hunt with, not those solitary toes you have."

B. J. shook her mane, "These are NOT solitary toes. They are hooves."

Zeke, peering around me snarled. "Well, we can grip the ground, go up and down hillsides with ease, and find and point birds."

B. J. walked towards us. "My legs and hooves enable me to gallop and glide over the ground with ease and speed to find birds."

"You may be able to gallop to find the birds," I barked. "But, you need to stop, point them, and wait for our hunter. Otherwise you would end up 'flushing' them and they would fly away."

Zeke's chest puffed up like a pumpkin and he began shaking. He growled. "You have a tail that is bushy and too long to point. Our tails are short, easy to point with, and we don't get them caught in the brush. They stick straight up in the tall grass so the Great One can find us."

B. J. lowered her head, coming closer to Zeke. She whinnied. "I use my tail to get those nasty horse flies off of me. Can you do that with your short tails?"

I looked at Zeke. "She has a point. There is no way we can do that with our short tails."

Zeke, barked as he moved back more. "How come your neck is so long? Besides, I never heard of a hunting horse."

B. J. tired of Zeke's questions, munched some more grass before answering. "The length of my neck enables me to find grass on both sides of the fence, and it's easier to sneak a snack or two in the barn."

Zeke, Deacon, and I growled at B. J. I looked behind me and realized if we didn't stop backing up, we would end up right in the Other One's newly planted vegetable garden with all those young tomato plants. B. J. tired of hearing Zeke, Deacon, and me bark, bolted towards us. Deacon and I ran to the side. Alas, Zeke didn't.

CRUNCH THROUGH THE GARDEN

Zeke started shaking all over and you could hear his teeth chattering. Backing up, he tripped over a rock, and landed in the vegetable garden. The Other One had decided that the best place for the garden was in the north pasture. That belief indeed was unfortunate. She hadn't figured on Zeke and B. J. in her garden.

A young green snapping turtle just happened to be looking for his lunch right then, and Zeke was on the menu. The turtle fastened its mouth on Zeke's short tail. Zeke leaped and bounced through the garden. At the same time, you could hear his high-pitched bark which sounded like *yelp, yelp.*

B. J. galloped through the vegetable garden chasing Zeke. It was quite a sight. Her hooves went CLOP, CLOP, CRUNCH, CRUNCH. Zeke continued to jump, bounce, and howl with B. J. nipping at his legs.

"There go the tomatoes." I barked. Deacon, splattered with mud from B. J. and Zeke romping through the garden, sat next to me, shook his head, and watched the scene unfold.

Eventually, the turtle lost its hold, dropped to the ground and crawled away. B. J. stopped galloping, and Zeke, Deacon, and I decided to hide for a while. In the end, the vegetable garden was ruined, B. J. was in the pasture, and Zeke was in the dog house.

THE RACE

For days, Zeke, Deacon, and I would lie by the oak tree and watch as the Great One spent time with B. J. – instead of us. One day I heard soft whistles and chatters of *wee, click, wee, click,* coming from the dove's nest where the cowbird was. I glanced up and saw our cowbird watching B. J. and our hunter. But, I also noticed three small cowbirds peering over the top of the nest.

"Zeke, look up. The cowbird has a family."

Zeke whined. "I don't care about the cowbird and its family. Look at all the time our hunter spends with B. J. Ever since she came, he acts like we aren't even around."

I yelped softly. "Zeke, the Great One is working with B. J. to make her part of our family. He still needs us to help him hunt quail birds. B. J. can't creep through the tall grass and find quail. Why, she would scare them off!"

One day, Zeke and I crept close to the barn to spy on B. J. She was eating grass around the barn. We were still afraid of B. J. We sneaked up behind the tractor and peered around to watch her.

Zeke's eyes got big like the dog toys we chew on. He trembled and whispered, "Do you think she eats dogs, Doc?"

"No, all we've seen her do is eat grass or be ridden by our hunter." I felt I needed to explain more to Zeke. "Look at her long neck. It isn't very efficient for eating. Our necks are short, so the chow goes straight to our stomach. It must take forever for the grass to get to her stomach. How can she hunt or be ridden when she's hungry all the time?" Zeke, understood eating, and seemed to accept my explanation. He simply nodded.

B. J. trotted off to the barn. Zeke and I followed from a distance. We watched her go into a horse stall. She put her head and long neck through the front end of the stall and started eating our dog chow from the barrel.

Zeke, angry about that, strutted right up to B. J. He clenched his teeth, then growled. "How dare you eat our dog chow."

B. J. stopped eating, brought her head up, backed out of the stall, and stared directly at Zeke and me.

Zeke was startled. His mouth dropped wide open. I spotted his teeth. They sparkled in the sunlight.

I didn't want B. J. to think two well-bred German Shorthaired Pointers with great pedigrees (papers about our ancestors and us) were afraid of a race horse. Therefore, I casually stepped towards her, then barked. "Ah, er, we wanted to welcome you to our family. We thought you might be interested in how we take care of the people."

B. J.'s large nostrils flexed in and out, as she pawed the ground and whinnied. "I also have lived with many people. As a famous race horse, I know how to handle them!" She turned away from us and started eating our chow again.

Zeke snapped his mouth shut, gathered his courage, then howled with his loudest bark. "HORSES DON'T EAT DOG CHOW!"

B. J. twirled around, swished her tail, and snorted. "Is that so? Well, I'm a horse, and I'll eat what I want to. I have to keep up my strength."

At that point, I inched closer to her. *What B. J. said sounded exactly like Zeke! They can't be related.*

Zeke peered around me and faced B. J. His hair stood straight up on his back and he snarled. "I'll race you once around the north pasture and whoever wins gets to eat all the extra dog chow in the barn."

B. J. became jittery, pawed the ground, trotted up to Zeke, and neighed, "Tomorrow when the sun is straight up, we'll race."

I couldn't believe what my dog ears heard. Our Zeke wanting to *race* a race horse. Zeke has always told me, "Doc, I walk with the Great One when we hunt so that I can pace myself. That gives me the energy to retrieve the birds you find."

That night around the kennels, the entire hacienda was howling about the great race the next day. The birds heard the pack. They told the deer. The deer told the coyotes. The coyotes told the mice, rabbits, gophers, frogs, crickets, and grasshoppers. Before the night was over all the animals near the Lazy Dog Hacienda knew about the race! Most of the pack couldn't believe Zeke challenged a famous race horse. They knew Zeke didn't like to run. Besides, his run was like a short walk for the rest of us.

During the middle of the night, I heard Zeke whimpering to Deacon. I looked over at the next run. Zeke trembled. "You know Doc, I've decided that Deacon should race in my place. He really enjoys running. I need to save myself for when we go hunting in the fall. Besides, I don't feel well."

"You don't say, Zeke." *You're really afraid you will lose.* I made a short bark of laughter, then yawned and went to sleep.

Race day came. Noon is the hottest part of the day at the Lazy Dog Hacienda. The pond was in the middle of the north pasture and had the best view of the race. You could hear the buzzing of the grasshoppers as they hopped through the grass trying to get to the pond with the frogs. The birds, deer, coyotes, mice, gophers, crickets, and the rest of the pack all gathered around the edge of the pond. This would be the biggest race the Lazy Dog Hacienda ever had.

Deacon, Zeke, and I trotted over to the pasture. It sure didn't look like Zeke was sick. He wasn't coughing. There was B. J., waiting for us in the shade under our oak tree. She was staring not at us, but at the cowbird who was still in the nest. A flock of young cowbirds were peering from the top of the nest.

Zeke's mouth dropped open showing the silver from his teeth as they sparkled in the glow of the sun. Almost as if on cue, Zeke started coughing *CAK, CAK, CAK.* Usually Zeke only coughs when the thought of strenuous exercise is mentioned. Gasping for breath, Zeke barked, "I have this terrible cough. . ."

"Oh, I see, you're afraid you won't win against a race horse!" B. J. shook her mane, and twisted her head around to nibble her side where flies were biting.

"I'M NOT AFRAID," Zeke snarled. "Deacon will race in my place since I'm coughing so much. The Great One likes for me to save my strength for hunting season." Zeke's eyes darted from B. J. to Deacon.

I glanced at Deacon as he barked, "it's a good thing I just finished eating those binders on the horse books. I read all about race horses and racing." Deacon, looked up at the cowbirds as they were suddenly chattering. *What was that all about?*

B. J. pulled her lips back from her teeth. She showed a toothy grin. "We'll start from this oak tree. We'll go around the pasture, and back to the oak tree. The cowbird will start the race. I get to eat all the dog chow if I win, agreed?"

"We agree." I barked as Zeke's teeth chattered. He glanced up at B. J.

B. J. and Deacon lined up under the oak tree. Zeke and I were panting because it was so hot. We decided to move near the pond so we could see the race better, and be under the shade of trees. The cowbird perched in the nest of the oak tree yelled, "when I shout *wee, click,* start running."

Suddenly, we heard *coo, coo*, and many doves appeared including the one that was kicked out of its nest by the cowbird. They swooped down and kicked the cowbird out of the nest, but left the young cowbirds in the nest. I guess they didn't have a problem with them. The flustered cowbird shrieked *wee, click, wee, click,* and landed on B. J.'s mane, grasping her mane with its toes. Startled, B. J. reared up and lunged forward like a rocket. Deacon sprang after her. I watched as they rounded the first curve.

B. J.'s solitary toes and long strides left our three-legged Deacon behind. You could barely see the cowbird upside down, its toes desperately holding on to B. J.'s mane. By the second turn, Deacon was catching up, B. J.'s coat was damp with sweat, and the cowbird dangled by only ONE toe.

B. J. neighed as she started around the third corner. "I'm going to win".

"No, you aren't," Zeke howled back. He rushed towards B. J. That was a mistake! B. J.'s back hooves kicked something up from the ground, right in front of Zeke that looked very big and very dark.

Horse poop! Sure enough, Zeke fell and rolled in it. B. J. and Deacon left Zeke in a cloud of dust. I heard Zeke cry out *yip, yip, yip.*

With a burst of speed Deacon roared by B. J. The animals cheered. B. J. galloped as fast as she could. She leapt in front of Deacon. Huffing and puffing, Deacon used all of his strength to catch up with B. J. They turned down the home stretch, nose to nose, solitary toes to front paws. B. J. inched in front of Deacon. They were only a few dog lengths from the finish line.

B. J.'s victory seemed certain – until the unexpected happened. She tried to nip Deacon's right front leg with her teeth. B. J. missed that, so she tried for the back leg. Unlucky, for her, Deacon didn't have that leg so B J. stumbled forward. The cowbird lost its grip, and plunged to the ground directly in front of her! B. J. lost her balance, tripped over the cowbird, and ended up falling to the ground. Deacon crossed the finish line in front of B. J. and won the race.

B. J. limped up to Deacon, head hung down and cried out *hee, hee.* "Deacon, you are a race dog." All the animals in the north pasture cheered our three-legged Deacon.

I guess Zeke didn't understand that the cheering was for Deacon. Zeke held his head high as he walked up to us. He had quite an aroma and his ticked coat was a solid dark brown.

Deacon, always the nice one, shared the extra dog chow with us. He even let B. J. sneak a few bites! The chow was moved to the garage when our people noticed it was disappearing. The pack and B. J. lost weight.

Zeke spent days grooming his ticked coat to get the smelly manure out.

The cowbird, distressed by being kicked out of the dove's nest and falling off B. J., left the neighborhood. Stories were circulated about a strange cowbird that wouldn't leave the ground. The young cowbirds were raised by the doves.

The Great One lost interest in B. J. when she took a bite out of the upholstery in his old red truck. We heard B. J. was shipped to new owners in Texas.

Hunting season arrived, and attention was bestowed on us again. The animals at the Lazy Dog Hacienda would never forget the greatest race - hunting dog against a race horse!